SPOTLIGHT ON ECOLOGY AND LIFE SCIENCE

# ANIMAL MIGRATION



HOLDEN STRAUSS

PowerKiDS press.

NEW YORK

Published in 2017 by The Rosen Publishing Group, Inc.
29 East 21st Street, New York, NY 10010



Editor: Caitie McAneney
Book Design: Michael Flynn
Interior Layout: Tanya Dellaccio

Photo Credits: Cover Gail Johnson/Shutterstock.com; p. 5 Art Wolfe/Getty Images; p. 6 EastVillage Images/Shutterstock.com; p. 7 mdd/Shutterstock.com; p. 9 (main) Atosan/Shutterstock.com; p. 9 (inset) Stephen J Krasemann/Getty Images; p. 11 (main) Regis Vincent/Shutterstock.com; p. 11 (inset) Buyenlarge/Getty Images; p. 12 Joost van Uffelen/Shutterstock.com; p. 13 Catmando/Shutterstock.com; p. 15 (main) Yva Momatiuk & John Eastcott/Minden Pictures/Getty Images; p. 15 (inset) R_Koopmans/Getty Images; p. 16 HADI ZAHER/Getty Images; p. 17 Auscape/Getty Images; p. 19 (main) Michael Warwick/Shutterstock.com; p. 19 (inset) Florilegius/SSPL/Getty Imgaes; p. 21 (main) Stefan Christmann/Getty Images; p. 21 (inset) vladsilver/Shutterstock.com.

Library of Congress Cataloging-in-Publication Data

Names: Strauss, Holden.
Title: Animal migration / Holden Strauss.
Description: New York : PowerKids Press, 2017. | Series: Spotlight on ecology and life science | Includes index.
Identifiers: ISBN 9781499425796 (pbk.) | ISBN 9781499425826 (library bound) | ISBN 9781499425802 (6 pack)
Subjects: LCSH: Animal migration--Juvenile literature.
Classification: LCC QL754.S745 2017 | DDC 591.56'8--d23

Manufactured in the United States of America

CPSIA Compliance Information: Batch #BW17PK For further information contact Rosen Publishing, New York, New York at 1-800-237-9932.

# CONTENTS

# CHAPTER ONE

# TIME TO MIGRATE!

Animal migrations provide some of the most amazing scenes in nature. Many animals migrate, or move from one region to another, in packs of close family members. Others migrate with thousands of other animals. Where are those animals going? Why do they leave their homes?

Some animals migrate before winter months when the weather starts to get cold. You may look up in the fall and see geese flying south. These animals are looking for warmer places to spend the winter. Other animals migrate to find food or water. This is especially true for animals that live in very dry areas. Their **habitat** doesn't have resources readily available, so they have to move around a lot. Animals also migrate to mate, or come together to make babies. Let's take a look at some of the world's most famous migrating animals!

Bar-tailed godwits make the longest nonstop flying migration of any animal on Earth. Some fly more than 7,000 miles (11,265.4 km) from Alaska to New Zealand without a break!

# CHAPTER TWO

# THE GREAT MIGRATION

Wildebeests in southeastern Africa make a huge migration each year. It's considered one of the wonders of the natural world. Wildebeests are hoofed animals that are also called gnus. Each year, around 1.5 million wildebeests, as well as zebras and Thomson's gazelles, migrate in a loop around the Serengeti Plain.

People come from around the world to see the great wildebeest migration.

The Serengeti Plain is an **ecosystem** found in east-central Africa. It stretches from Tanzania to Kenya. Much of the land is covered in grass or trees. It's warm and dry much of the year, but there are two rainy seasons. The animals keep moving toward better food and water sources, completing a loop each year.

The journey is very dangerous, or unsafe. Around 250,000 wildebeests may die each year. Predators hunt tired, young, or weak wildebeests. Other wildebeests die of thirst or hunger. They have to travel through lands full of lions and hyenas and cross rivers full of crocodiles waiting for a bite.

# CHAPTER THREE

# ELEPHANTS ON THE MOVE

The African elephant is another African animal that migrates to find food and water. African elephants are the largest land animals on Earth. They need to eat a lot of food to survive. In fact, an adult African elephant can eat nearly 300 pounds (136 kg) of food each day.

African elephants sometimes live in rain forests. Others live in dry desert land, such as the Sahel desert in Mali. When it's very dry, an elephant herd must roam around looking for food and water. Female elephants and young elephants often migrate together, while male elephants often roam alone. Herds usually have between 10 and 20 members. Sometimes they have as many as 500 members.

Male elephants migrate each year to find females to mate with. This usually happens in the spring. After the elephants mate, the male elephant leaves the herd and goes his own way.

Elephants are a one-of-a-kind animal. However, long ago, similar animals called woolly mammoths roamed North America.

Migrating in groups helps keep elephants safe. Elephants form strong bonds with one another.

# CHAPTER FOUR

# AMAZING ARCTIC TERNS

The arctic tern is a small, sharp-winged bird with a black cap of feathers. This bird may be tiny, but it holds the record for the longest total migration of any animal on Earth.

Every year, arctic terns fly a zigzag path between Greenland in the north and Antarctica in the south. During just one migration, this little bird may fly nearly 60,000 miles (96,560 km)!

Scientists used to think the arctic tern flew a much shorter distance. However, they placed **miniature** tracking tools around the legs of a few arctic terns. They found that terns migrate more than two times farther than they'd estimated. They also learned terns take a long break to rest and eat. The terns' zigzag path follows wind patterns, which saves energy. The birds always fly with the wind and not against it.

Scientists believe arctic terns migrate to find food.

# CHAPTER FIVE

# HUGE HUMPBACK WHALES

Humpback whales are some of the largest animals on Earth. They can grow to more than 60 feet (18.3 m) long and weigh more than 40 tons (36.3 mt). They eat lots of tiny sea animals, such as **plankton**, small fish, and krill.

Humpback whales migrate to find enough food. In the summer, they swim to Arctic and Antarctic waters. In the

Humpback whales' calls often sound like songs. Scientists think each sound has a purpose.

winter, they swim to **tropical** waters closer to the equator. Humpback whales often mate and give birth in these tropical areas. They stay close to the shore where there are lots of tiny ocean creatures to eat.

These whales migrate in groups called pods. Mothers swim close to their babies. They make calls to one another to **communicate** and help the pod stick together. Each year, humpback whales migrate about 3,000 miles (4,828 km).

# CHAPTER SIX

# SALMON SWIMMING UPSTREAM

Have you ever seen a fish swimming upstream? The sockeye salmon is known to swim against the water's current when it migrates.

Sockeye salmon are a kind of Pacific salmon. Adults live in the sea, but they have babies in freshwater. So, the sockeyes swim upriver from the salty sea to freshwater lakes. There, they mate and lay their eggs. The parent sockeyes soon die, but their young stay in the lake where they were born for up to three years. Then they head to the sea, where they eat lots of tiny ocean animals. They come back after a few years to lay their own eggs.

Sockeyes actually change color during migration. When a sockeye lives in the sea, its coloring is silver or blue with black spots. When the sockeye migrates upstream, its head turns green and its body turns red.

SOCKEYE SALMON EGGS

Sockeye salmon migrate from areas of the northern Pacific Ocean to areas farther inland. Some swim upriver to areas of Japan, while others swim upriver to lakes in the U.S. Pacific Northwest.

# CHAPTER SEVEN

# ATTACK OF THE CRABS!

Christmas Island is located in the Indian Ocean, and it's an Australian territory. Its name is fitting, as this island is decorated in red each year during its rainy season. That's when tens of millions of red crabs migrate across the island. They make the journey each year across roads and forests and rocky coastline. Roads close to let the crabs through. They're on a mission!

Crabs need to make it safely to the water to **hydrate** and mate. People build "crab crossings" to help the crabs along.

These red crabs crawl out of the forest, where they spend most of the year. Then they travel to the coast, where they mate and lay their eggs. The eggs hatch when they touch salt water. The baby crabs, called larvae, are soon washed out to sea. They grow until they look more like small adult crabs and then leave the water. The young crabs migrate to the forest to finish growing into adults.

# CHAPTER EIGHT

# MILLIONS OF MONARCHS

Imagine going outside and seeing millions of monarch butterflies. These orange-and-black butterflies are North American bugs that migrate like birds. In the winter, they fly south, and in the spring, they fly back north. They can travel up to 100 miles (160.9 km) each day to make their long journey. Some fly up to 3,000 miles (4,828 km) to escape the cold!

Monarch butterflies have a great sense of direction. Every year, their trip south is the first trip for that **generation** of butterflies. However, somehow they know where to go! Monarchs from eastern North America fly south to Mexico. They like to live in oyamel fir trees in the mountains. Western North American monarchs spend their winter in Southern California. Monarchs then lay their eggs. The eggs hatch and the new butterflies fly north later in the spring.

Monarch butterflies go to the same places, and even the same trees, each year. How do they know where to fly? It's one of nature's great wonders.

# CHAPTER NINE

# PENGUINS MARCHING

Penguins are just one of the many kinds of birds that migrate. However, these birds can't fly. Instead, emperor penguins waddle about 50 miles (80.5 km) a year across the ice sheets of Antarctica.

Emperor penguins are the largest penguins in the world. They have black heads and wings and white bellies. They are built for the cold weather and they stand close together to keep one another warm. Female penguins lay eggs, but male penguins take care of the eggs.

Female penguins migrate to hunt. They travel for up to two months to the ocean and back. There, they feast on fish and other marine creatures. They return to their home with their bellies full. They meet their hatched chicks and feed them food from their own stomachs. Then, they let the males go on their own migration to the ocean to eat their fill.

Male emperor penguins keep eggs warm while the females are away. Males and females work together as a team to raise their family and find food!

# CHAPTER TEN

# HOW CAN WE HELP?

When animals migrate, they're looking for a certain kind of land, weather, food, or water source. For example, monarch butterflies traveling to certain trees in Mexico expect those same trees to be there each year. Elephants depend on their usual sources of water and food. Animal migrations suffer when people destroy natural habitats.

People create pollution that can **disrupt** migration and harm animals who eat garbage by mistake. Migrating sea turtles can get caught in fishing nets. Man-made lights hurt night-flying birds that normally use the moon and stars to **navigate**. Sound pollution in the water can disrupt whale communication. **Climate change** has affected water temperatures, so marine animals have to take new paths while migrating.

People can also help solve some of the problems facing migrating animals. Tracking tools and **drones** help us learn about migration paths. There's much more to learn about these amazing animals and their journeys!

# GLOSSARY

**climate change** (KLY-meht CHANJ) Long-term change in Earth's weather, caused partly by human activities such as burning oil and natural gas.

**communicate** (kuh-MYU-nuh-kayt) To share ideas and feelings through sounds and motions.

**disrupt** (dihs-RUHPT) To cause something to be unable to continue in a normal way.

**drone** (DROHN) A pilotless aircraft.

**ecosystem** (EE-koh-sis-tuhm) A natural community of living and nonliving things.

**generation** (jen-uh-RAY-shun) A group of individuals born about the same time.

**habitat** (HAA-buh-tat) The natural place where an animal or plant lives.

**hydrate** (HY-drayt) To add water to the body.

**miniature** (MIH-nee-uh-chur) A smaller form of something.

**navigate** (NAA-veh-gayt) To find one's way.

**plankton** (PLANK-tehn) A tiny plant or animal that floats in the ocean.

**tropical** (TRAH-pih-kuhl) Warm and wet regions of the world located close to the equator.

# INDEX



# PRIMARY SOURCE LIST

**Page 9**
Woolly mammoth skeleton. Reconstructed fossilized bone. Now kept in Royal Tyrrell Museum of Palaeontology, Alberta, Canada.

**Page 11**
Illustration of an Arctic tern. Based on an image painted by John James Audubon. From *Birds of America* by John James Audubon. Published in London, England, and Edinburgh, Scotland, between 1827 and 1838.

**Page 18**
Hand-colored engraving showing a monarch butterfly, red cracker butterfly, and doris longwing butterfly. Created by Fournier based on an illustration by Oudart from Charles d'Orbigny's *Dictionnaire Universel d'Histoire Naturelle*. Published in Paris, France, in 1849.

# WEBSITES

Due to the changing nature of Internet links, PowerKids Press has developed an online list of websites related to the subject of this book. This site is updated regularly. Please use this link to access the list: www.powerkidslinks.com/sels/migra